This title was originally catalogued by the Library of Congress as follows: Seuss, Dr. I wish that I had duck feet, by Theo. LeSieg. Illustrated by B. Tobey. New York, Beginner Books [1965] 64 p. col. illus. 24 cm. "B-40." I. Tobey, Barney, illus. II. Title. PZ7.G2719 I 65-21211 ISBN 0-394-80040-0 ISBN 0-394-90040-5 (lib. bdg.)

I WISH
that I had
DUCK FEET

by Theo. LeSieg

Illustrated by B TOBEY-

BEGINNER BOOKS   A Division of Random House, Inc.

I wish
that I had duck feet.
And I can tell you why.
You can splash around in duck feet.
You don't have to keep them dry.

3

I wish that I had duck feet.

No more shoes!

No shoes for me!

The man down at the shoe store

would not have my size, you see.

If I had two duck feet,
I could laugh at Big Bill Brown.
I would say, "YOU don't have duck feet!
These are all there are in town!"

I think it would be very good
to have them when I play.
Only kids with duck feet on
can ever play this way.

BUT . . .

My mother would not like them.

She would say, "Get off my floor!"

She would say, "You take your duck feet

and you take them out that door!

"Don't ever come in here again
with duck feet on. Now, DON'T."
SO . . .
I guess I can't have duck feet.
I would like to. But I won't.

11

SO . . .

If I can't have duck feet,

I'll have something else instead . . .

Say!

I know what!

I wish I had

two horns up on my head!

I wish I had two deer horns.

They would be a lot of fun.

Then I could wear

ten hats up there!

Big Bill can just wear one.

I think they would
be very good
to have when I play ball.
Then nobody could stop me.
No, sir! Nobody at all!

18

My horns could carry
books and stuff
like paper, pens and strings
and apples for my teacher
and a lot of other things!

19

BUT . . .
If I had
big deer horns,
I would never
get a ride.

20

I could never ride the school bus.
I could never get inside!

AND SO . . .

I won't have deer horns.

I'll have something else instead.

I wish I had a whale spout.

A whale spout on my head!

When days get hot

it would be good

to spout my spout in school.

And then Miss Banks
would say, "Thanks! Thanks!
You keep our school so cool."

I could play all day in summer.

I would never feel the heat.

I would beat Big Bill at tennis.

I would play him off his feet.

BUT . . .

My mother would not like it.

I know just what she would say:

"Not in the house!

You shut that off!

You take that spout away."

28

I know that she would tell me,
"I don't want that spout about!"
And when Mother
does not want a thing,
it's O—U—T. It's out!

AND SO . . .

I will not have one.

I don't wish to be a whale.

I think
it would be better
if I had
a long, long tail.

I wish I had a long, long tail.

Some day I will. I hope.

And then I'll show

the kids in town

new ways to jump a rope!

If I had a long, long tail
I know what I would like.
I would like to ride down State Street
pulling girls behind my bike.

I wish I had a long, long tail.
And I can tell you why.
I could hit a fly ten feet away
and hit him in the eye.

I know Miss Banks would like this.
She would smile and she would say,
"No other boy in town can hit
a fly so far away."

BUT . . .

If I had a long, long tail,

I know that Big Bill Brown

would tie me in a tree!

He would!

Then how would I get down?

I don't think that I would like it
with my tail tied in a tree.
The more I think about it . . . NO!
No long, long tail for me.

AND SO . . .

If I can't have a tail,

I'll have a long, long nose!

A nose just like an elephant's,

the longest nose that grows.

I wish I had a long, long nose

and I can tell you why.

I think it would

be very good

to get at things up high.

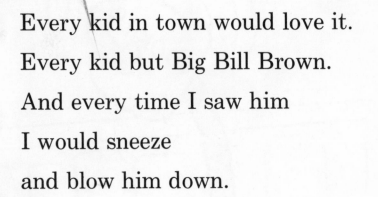

Every kid in town would love it.
Every kid but Big Bill Brown.
And every time I saw him
I would sneeze
and blow him down.

KERCHOO!

43

Say!
I could help the firemen!
My nose would be just right.
I could help them put out fires
a hundred times a night.

Oh, I would do a lot of things
that no one ever did.
And everyone in town would say,
"Just watch that long-nose kid!"

47

BUT . . .

If I had a long, long nose,

I know what Dad would do.

My dad would make me wash the car!

The house and windows, too!

My dad would make me work all day
and wash things with that hose!
I guess it would not be so good
to have a long, long nose.

NOW . . .

Let me think about it.

All these things I want are bad.

And so I wish . . .

I wish . . . I wish . . .

What DO I wish I had? . . .

I know what!

I know just what!

I know just what to do!

I WISH THAT I HAD ALL THOSE

THINGS!

I'd be a Which-What-Who!

If I could be a Which-What-Who,
I'd jump high in the air.
I'd splash and spout
and run about.
I'd give the town a scare!

BUT . . .

The people would not like it.

They would be so scared, I bet,

they would call the town policemen.

They would catch me in a net!

They would put me in the zoo house
with my horns and nose and feet.
And hay, just hay,
two times a day
is all I'd get to eat.

I think I would be very sad
when people came to call.
SO . . .
I don't think
a Which-What-Who
would be much fun at all.

AND SO . . .

I think
there are some things
I do not wish to be.

And that is why
I think that I
just wish to be like ME.

989

94
994
1995

997

998